P9-DFD-485

# PEARL AND SQUIRREL GIVE THANKS

By Cassie and Ryan Ehrenberg

Orchard Books
New York
An Imprint of Scholastic Inc.

Library of Congress Cataloging-in-Publication Data available

ISBN 978-1-338-59209-2

10 9 8 7 6 5 4 3 2 1        20 21 22 23 24

Printed in Malaysia 108
First edition, September 2020
Book design by Rae Crawford

Inside a box beside the old corner store live Pearl and Squirrel.

Pearl loves to play.
Her favorite place is the park.
That's where she met her best buddy, Squirrel.

Squirrel can be shy, but he's very smart.
He likes to read and learn new things.

Together, they roam the city looking for adventure.

One morning, Pearl wakes up extra hungry.
"Get up, Squirrel!" she shouts.
"Just a few more minutes!" groans Squirrel.
Pearl nudges him. "C'mon, I'm hungry!"

They head out to the park, looking for something tasty to eat.

Squirrel would like to eat something fancy.

Pearl is much less picky.

They see Stan, the food cart man.
He's always kind and happy to share.
"There you are!" he calls. "I have something for you."

"A special treat for Thanksgiving."

Squirrel eats slowly.

Pearl does not.

Pearl wonders what Thanksgiving is.
"Thanksgiving is when you share what you're thankful for
with family and friends," Stan explains.
"I'm always thankful to spend time with you two."
Pearl gives Stan a goodbye lick before they continue to the park.

"Hey, Squirrel, let's try Thanksgiving!
We can point out all the things we're thankful for!" Pearl says.
Squirrel responds with a shrug.

They walk through yards.
"I'm thankful for fetch!" Pearl calls.

They walk through playgrounds.
"I'm thankful for jump rope!" Pearl yells.

At last, they enter the park.
"I'm thankful for this fountain to swim in!" says Pearl.
"Yuck, it looks dirty," Squirrel replies.

They reach the meadow.
"I'm thankful for new friends," Pearl calls.
"I'd rather sit," Squirrel says.

"I'm thankful for this cuddly nap spot,"
Pearl says sleepily. Squirrel just nods.

# CRACK!

They wake to rain pouring from the sky.
Pearl watches as people take their pets and leave the park in a hurry.
"We better get home!" Squirrel shouts.

The streets are cold and wet. Pearl and Squirrel shiver in the damp air.
For the first time that day, Pearl feels sad.
She wishes they had a real home.
"I'd be thankful to live here. Nice and warm, with hot food each day,"
Pearl says with a sigh.

When they get back home, their box is already soaked.
Pearl curls up in the driest corner.
"I don't feel very thankful anymore," she says quietly.

"You know what, Pearl?" Squirrel asks. "You're my best friend.
No matter where we live, I'm most thankful for you."
Pearl smiles wide. "Squirrel! You're doing Thanksgiving!"

Pearl and Squirrel cuddle together and try to stay dry.
But soon, the soggy box is breaking apart.

Shivering in the cold, the two suddenly
hear footsteps getting closer. They look out to see . . .

# . . . Stan!

"There you are! I've been looking all over for you two," he says with a smile. "I thought you might be cold on a night like this. Want to join me for a nice Thanksgiving dinner?"

Pearl jumps into Stan's arms and Squirrel cuddles into his shirt pocket.

Stan helps them get clean and dry.

"I'm thankful for soap," Squirrel says.

"I'm thankful for towels!" Pearl shouts.

Next, they sit down for a
tasty holiday dinner made
just for them.

"You know," says Stan, "I have plenty of room here
if you'd like to stay and live with me."
Pearl and Squirrel jump up and give him a big hug.

"I'll take that as a yes," Stan
says with a laugh.

Pearl and Squirrel are thankful to have a new family and their own place to belong.